◀ Barti and Bel ▶

LOOK for a BOOK

◀ Suzanne Carpenter ▶

To Mairwen, Barti and Bel's guardian angel

Published in 2006 by Pont Books, an imprint of
Gomer Press, Llandysul, Ceredigion SA44 4JL

ISBN 1 84323 714 8
ISBN-13 9781843237143

Thank you to Rhondda Cynon Taf Schools Library
Service for the photograph on page 2-3

This book is published with the financial support of the
Welsh Books Council.

Printed in Wales at
Gomer Press, Llandysul, Ceredigion

LIBRARY

We'd like to borrow some books today –

What shall we choose to take away?

Help us search, help us look –

Which will be our favourite book?

Make a cake

Find minibeasts

See an x-ray

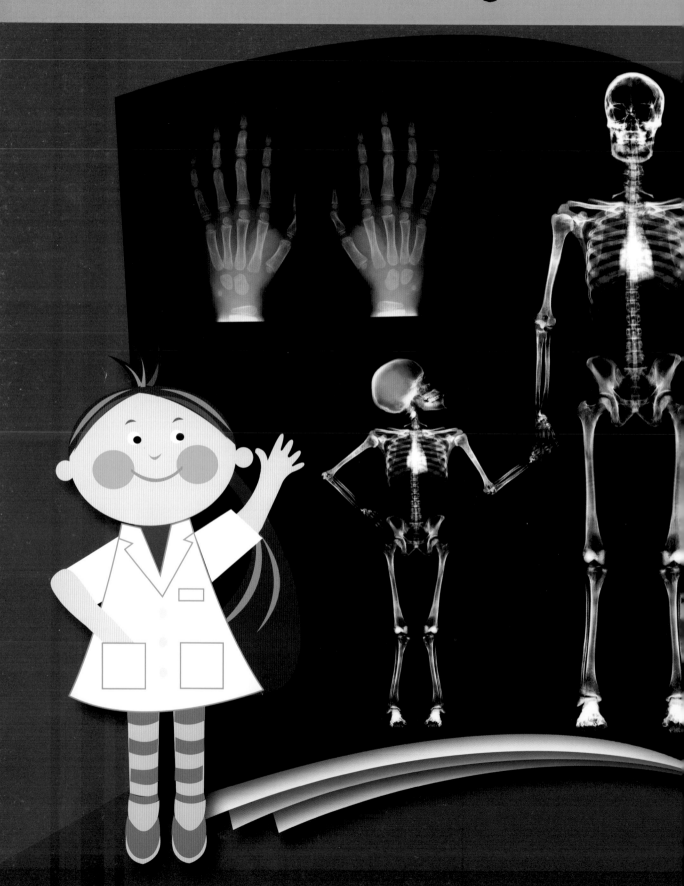

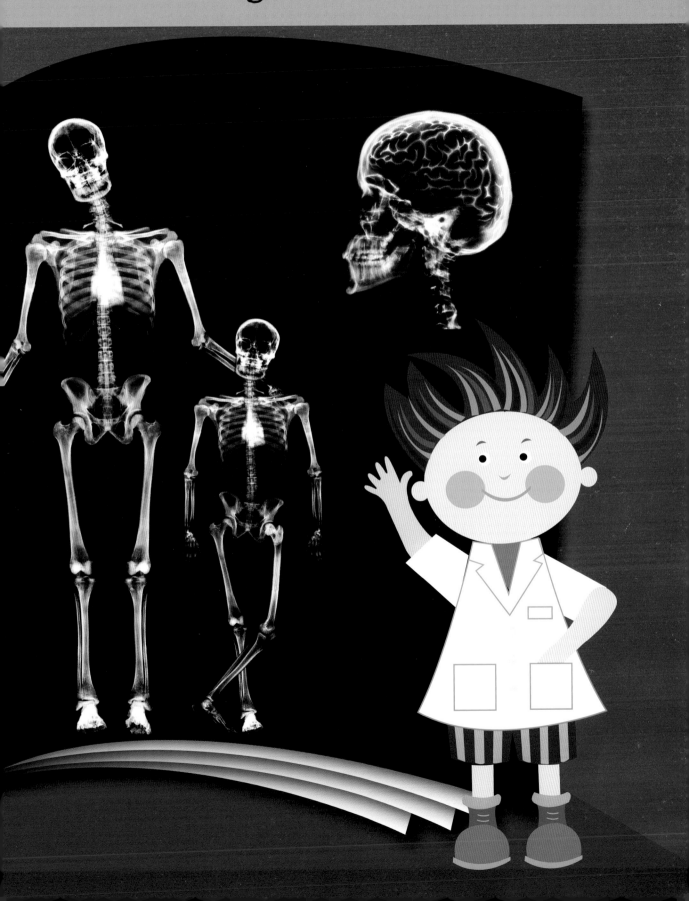

Move around

Wear a mask

See the stars

Plant some seeds

Trace the tracks

Milk a cow

Swim with fishes

Splash in the sun

splash in the rain

Jump on a bus

We've found a bagful of books we can borrow

Two for today and three for tomorrow

Books that take us to lots of new places

Teach us new skills and put smiles on our faces

We'll see you next week when we'll be back to look

On the library shelves for a BRILLIANT BOOK.